Once Upon A Dream

UK Dreamers

Edited By Shariqua Ahmed

First published in Great Britain in 2017 by:

Young Writers
Remus House
Coltsfoot Drive
Peterborough
PE2 9BF
Telephone: 01733 890066
Website: www.youngwriters.co.uk

All Rights Reserved
Book Design by Tim Christian
© Copyright Contributors 2017
SB ISBN 978-1-78820-862-8
Printed and bound in the UK by BookPrintingUK
Website: www.bookprintinguk.com
YB0319CZ

FOREWORD

Welcome to 'Once Upon a Dream – UK Dreamers'.

For our latest competition for primary school pupils, we asked dreamers from primary schools all over the country to write poems inspired by their dreams. This could mean the topsy-turvy imaginative world we visit each night, or the goals we have for the future. Some writers also chose to delve into the creepy world of nightmares!

Dreams provide a rich and varied source of inspiration, as is clear from the diverse and entertaining poems we received. It was great to see how the writers had fun with the theme and let their imaginations run riot, as well as getting to grips with poetic forms such as the acrostic. Inside this collection you will find poems about everything from flying to football, with lots of chocolate and candy lands along the way.

Picking a favourite from the anthology was tough so well done to *Ornaigh McGrath Atkinson* who is the winning poet. I would also like to congratulate all the young writers featured in these pages, I hope it encourages you to keep following your writing dreams!

Shariqua Ahmed

CONTENTS

Winner:

Ornaigh McGrath Atkinson (10) -
SS Peter & Paul RC Primary   1
School, Redland

Independent Entries

Freya Rachel Povey	3
Alfie Brace (8)	4
Sophie Hegarty (10)	6
Eva Howlett (7)	7
Rina-Phoebe Adwoa Antwi-Agyei (6)	8
Lucy Elizabeth Heron (9)	9
Clara Ashing	10

Chad Vale Primary School, Edgbaston

Kupakwashe Z Nhara (8)	11
Sophie Kilroy (7)	12
Simar Kaur Bharya (8)	13

Herington House School, Hutton Mount

Chloe Tarbard (9)	14
Inaaya Anwar (9)	16
Taylor Stack (10)	18
Sam Bear (10)	19
Torin De Silva (9)	20
Romy Skarott (9)	21
Harry Clarke (10)	22
Dilan Kanagasabai (9)	23
Harry Toms (9)	24

Ludwell Primary School, Ludwell

Devon Charlotte Batho (11)	25

Northside Primary School, Northside

Josh Dixon (9)	27
Finlay Tweedie (8)	28
Ryan Fell (9)	29
Madison Pickering (9)	30
Thomas James Busby (9)	31
Aidan Lee Sharp (9)	32
Levi Earl (9)	33
Sonny Coulson (7)	34

SS Peter & Paul RC Primary School, Redland

Divina Sivajoti (10)	35
Katie Skiffington (10)	36
James Taylor (9)	38
Francesca Harvey (11)	40
Lily Loughlin (10)	41
Iris Taylor (10)	42
Rivie Tilly Bates	43
Geraldine Cross Rosales (10)	44
Katie Anna Watts (9)	45
Fergus McDonald (10)	46
Harry Harvey (9)	47
Lara Smith (10)	48
Theodore Bradwell (9)	49
Noah Scott (10)	50
Ryan Agenonga Prince Kanua (10)	51
Dylan Romero (10)	52
Aswin Jayan (9)	53

Ann Siby Stephen (10)	54
Oliver Clayton (9)	55
Kejti Dushaj (10)	56
Serena Alexandra Williams López (8)	57
Lola Cortes Hyland (9)	58
Edie Jeans (8)	59
Kevin Jerome (10)	60
Maeva Page Cotton (10)	61
Olivia Downie (8)	62
Antonia Garcia (9)	63
Steve Siby Stephen (10)	64
Anthony Shedov (10)	65
Bea Blackman (9)	66

St Vigor & St John CE Primary School, Chilcompton

Bethan Daly (10)	67
Jamie White (10)	68
Luke Mitchelmore (10)	70
Matt Denning Maggs (10)	71
Keira Maundrill (10)	72
Drew Reuben Box (11)	73
Izzy (10)	74
Leah (10)	75
Oliver Tibbs (10)	76
Noah Godber (11)	77
Sofia Amelie Todd (11)	78
James Peter Rideout (10)	79
Sebestyén Ciprián Tahin (10)	80
Grace May Pritchard (11)	81
Ben Taylor (11)	82
Finley Button (10)	83
Amber C Rayner (11)	84
Finley Lachlan Hunter-Clarke (10)	85
Toby Jones (11)	86
Holly Devlin (10)	87
Calvin Glover (11)	88
Dominika Eliza Kudyba (11)	89
Oliver Grace (11)	90

Whybridge Junior School, Rainham

Georgi O'Neill (11)	91
Hannah Pooley (10)	92
Sara Abdi Hassan Mahmuud (8)	94
Mariam Nuhu (11)	95
Lauren Hazell Daisey Patricia Hazell (10)	96
Elizabeth Durojaiye (8)	98
Nabila Hussain (9)	99
Chloé Barnard (8)	100
Mia Castello (9)	101
Annise Callender (9)	102
Jake Jackson (10)	103
Harry Fowler (9)	104
Harley Millard (9)	105
Luke Shepherd (10)	106
Kacie Flatt (9)	107
Camille Cumlajee (10)	108
Merve Fistikci (11)	109
Kevin Uka (10)	110
Jae Callender (8)	111
Kayleigh Mack (10)	112
Mia Fage (10)	113
Grace O'Connor (8)	114
Oluwanifemi Femi-Sanni (10)	115
Nelie Nunn (10)	116
Tommy Young (10)	117
Joseph Croft (10)	118
Kian Shay O'Riordan (10)	119
Bobby James Dancer (10)	120
Shreya Patel (9)	121
Martin Ganchev (10)	122
Archie Boys (9)	123
Katy Leigh Hart (10)	124
Mosope Braimoh (11)	125
Jude Smith (8)	126
Lily Bird (9)	127
George Wescombe (9)	128
Ruby Kitching (9)	129
Kian Boot (10)	130
Jesse-Jay Olney (10)	131
Denis Zegheru (9)	132

Max Chipperfield (8)	133
Joshua-James Leach (9)	134
Lara Crandle (8)	135
Oliver Maynard (9)	136
Holly Landers (10)	137
Ashton Hind (10)	138
Freya Barnard (10)	139
Chelvathurai Thanuzsan Thiruchelvam (9)	140
Erika Wilkins (9)	141
Sydney Stiffel (11)	142
Sadie Williams (9)	143
Sky Wood (9)	144
Jason Kissi Koranteng (10)	145
Alby Buttery (8)	146
Nanupriya Bhandari (8)	147
Rosie Casey (11)	148
Harry Casey (11)	149
Sumaya Yesmin (9)	150
Ava-May Watts (9)	151

THE POEMS

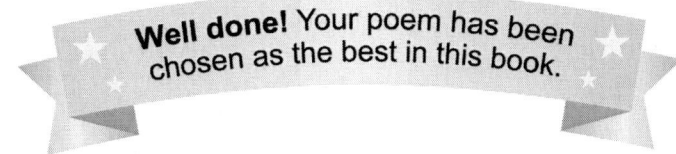

I Had A Dream Last Night...

I had a dream last night,
I was as free as a kite,
I battled a yeti with all my might,
It gave me such a horrendous fright.

I fought a werewolf, wand in hand,
I ventured right into Rowling's land,
I travelled to beaches, sprinkled with sand,
I was even part of the Beatles band!

I had a dream last night,
I was so carefree and light,
I didn't let the dream clouds out of my sight,
I was flying at such an alarming height!

I felt like a prisoner, being set free,
I had a dream, being seen only by me,
I was swung round by the Whomping Willow tree,
I was a circus leader in a great big marquee!

I had a dream last night,
I was warm and wrapped up tight, I had such a sight,
In the morning, I touched down from my flight;
I had a dream last night...

Ornaigh McGrath Atkinson (10)
SS Peter & Paul RC Primary School, Redland

Once Upon A...

This poem is like no other,
You'll get shivers down your spine,
Up your neck, in your eye,
It will be an experience like no other,
It all started in a little town,
My friend, called Chanelle,
She was bullied for a month,
Then she discovered a world of her own,
That she could go to when she was alone,
The world was made of candy,
Biscuits too,
The streams were made of hot chocolate,
With marshmallow boats,
People were lollies and pets.

The fakes, the bullies,
Their world was different,
From Chanelle's land,
Devils, ghosts, the worst of them...

Freya Rachel Povey

In The Dream Jar

Into the olive dream jar, the giant slammed a lime-coloured spotted caiman called Charlie who lives in the mossy leaves of Peru,
Into the pickle dream jar, the giant chucked the talking and singing of cicadas in the air,
Into the basil dream jar, the giant shut the menacing smell of a boggy swamp,
And the fruity taste of a butter-coloured banana.

Into the wine dream jar, the giant planted an arguing three-headed dog from Hogwarts,
Into the jam dream jar, the giant lay the jabberwocky's gigantic white canines,
Into the lavender dream jar, the giant located Grendel's fangs piercing a Viking's body,
And the whining of two greedy, fat goblins.

Into the dove-grey dream jar, the giant plummeted the magnetic force of Ethan Hunt climbing a secret organisation building,
Into the pencil-grey dream jar, the giant shoved James Bond against a couple of evil henchmen,
Into the iron-grey dream jar, is the quietness of a speechless spy,
And the mysterious creeping of a despicable criminal.
And a quiet cat living on a beautiful bristle with lush mauve coloured plums.

In the dream jar is a purple coloured juicy grape, from beautiful Bolivia,
In the dream jar is a lush fire-coloured dapple,
In the dream jar is a spooky place in South Africa,
And there is a secret odour with a magical entrance to Narnia.

Alfie Brace (8)

The Galaxy Far, Far Away

There is a galaxy far away,
And in that galaxy there are pixies and fairies,

And cakes that talk!

It's a magical place that's not in space,
It's in your imaginative brain,

Making up stories.

There are sweets galore,
And boyfriends, there's more,
And unicorns that can sing.

You can tell your secrets and no one hears,
All around you rainbows appear,
And you melt into peaceful happiness.

Sophie Hegarty (10)

Mad Monsters

M y monster is a magical monster who can do magic tricks
O n a disco ball that looks like traffic lights changing colour all the time
N o one was with me sadly, so I was alone
S cared like mice getting chased by cats
T he monsters have a party together
E very day
R aging music blasts as they all dance.

Eva Howlett (7)

The Clouds Falling

The clouds are falling!
Raindrops of colours falling out of the sky
Red, blue, green, pink, indigo
Falling, splashing, crashing
Running everywhere
Running so quickly
I can't see them
They are starting to fade away
They start to run slowly
The fade away
Soon they disappear
Nothing is left
I disappeared.

Rina-Phoebe Adwoa Antwi-Agyei (6)

Baboons

I wish I could see a baboon
I think baboons are special
I don't know why, they come running by.

Blue bums
Red noses
All different kinds of poses.

Baboons come in all different shapes and sizes,
Big or small, as thin as a pencil
Or as fat as a pig.

Lucy Elizabeth Heron (9)

Earth's Dream

Love,
a powerful source
when two hearts meet
and dance under a moonlit sky.
This is Earth's dream for her and Moon.
For their love to be as light as a feather
and as powerful as a laser.
That's Earth's
dream.

Clara Ashing

Football

Football, football
I love football
Kick the hard ball with my foot into the goal.
I am a good keeper, I save the kick.
I throw it to my teammates.
They take a hard shot and shoot it in the goal.
Yes!
What a goal!
I am a defender.
I tackle my opponent.
I pass it to my teammates.
He passed it to me.
And I shot it in the goal.

Kupakwashe Z Nhara (8)
Chad Vale Primary School, Edgbaston

The Sea

I was at the beach 'til I dived into the sea.
I went far and deep, 'til I saw something leap.
It was a frog fish of course, on a coral reef with lots of fish swimming underneath.
Late one night I found a jellyfish bloom with lots and lots and lots of gloom.
Then we slept in a kelp forest where we saw schools of flying fish.

Sophie Kilroy (7)
Chad Vale Primary School, Edgbaston

Owls

Sitting on the trees,
Very peacefully flying very high,
To reach the top of the sky,
Baby owls in the nest, waiting very long,
I guess.
Owls, owls flying high, glancing and dancing on the clouds,
People looking up to
Watch the owls fly high and high.

Simar Kaur Bharya (8)
Chad Vale Primary School, Edgbaston

Royal Golf

I stood outside the Queen's palace,
My pulse beating fast
I felt like I was being picked for Prime Minister,
All eyes were on me.

Suddenly the door opened,
And I was on a huge golf course
Who would have known?
The Queen has one in her drawing room.

I looked around at everything,
The long, dangling curtains
Shining in the sunlight,
Then I turned around.

And there was Prince William and
Guess what?
He asked me for a game of golf,
We set off onto hole one,
And stopped at hole four.

What a big, big surprise,
I beat him on all four.

We walked into the colossal palace,
And he offered me some tea.

We sat down at the table,
Guess who I was sitting next to,
The Queen!
I was nervous but at the same time,
I was as happy as a child on their holiday.

'Chloe, Chloe, wake up, you're late.'
There was my mum calling for me
I couldn't stop thinking that my dream wasn't real,
I thought I actually met the Queen.

Chloe Tarbard (9)
Herington House School, Hutton Mount

Candy Land

I was back in Candy Land,
Listening to a heavy rock band,
Until I found out
And without a doubt,
Mr Evil had escaped from prison
After the sun had risen.

He came swooping down,
And his face bore a frown,
He trapped me and my sidekick in gum,
But then out came his mum,
He flew far away
And didn't come back, even at the end of the day.

Then I saw a hand,
That pulled us out to land
We finally found Mr Evil
And his devilish little weevils.
We managed to frighten them all away
I hope they don't come back, I pray.

Obviously we won
And we got so much money, it weighed a tonne.
We were heroes once more,

And nobody remembered what had happened before
I finally woke up from my endless dream
Me and my sidekick were such a wonderful team.

Inaaya Anwar (9)
Herington House School, Hutton Mount

The Windy Storm

Bouncing on my trampoline with Dan,
Watched by an audience of my nan
We laughed and giggled very loud,
Then suddenly over came a stormy cloud.

Tree trunks arched in the wind,
Dan and I to the floor were pinned.
We staggered slowly from side to side,
But the wind howled, lashed and cried.

A sudden gust swept us up high,
Tossing us into the sultry sky.
Dan and I were terrified,
Where would we land? We were mystified.

Over the ant-like houses we flew,
Maybe we would land in Colchester zoo
But around we travelled for miles and miles,
Were we leaving the British Isles?

Down, down we dropped, I took a quick glance,
I think we may have been in France.
Now how on Earth were we going to get home?
If only I'd remembered to pick up my phone.

Taylor Stack (10)
Herington House School, Hutton Mount

The Easter Bunny

I wake up to find myself in a funny state of mind,
Surprised to find myself tied up in a bind,
I appear to be guarded by an Easter loving bunny,
This is rather curious, maybe it's quite funny.

The Easter bunny's fur is white
He really is a lovely sight.
He had dark black eyes and droopy ears,
I wonder how many eggs he had delivered to children over the years.

Usually I love to find the eggs he hides,
Between the bushes and trees outside.
Some are yellow, some are blue
I hope this year, he visits you.

However, this year I'm surprised to find
I won't be able to eat many eggs
If I'm still tied up in this bind!

Sam Bear (10)
Herington House School, Hutton Mount

Phone World

I was playing a game of Snow Cone,
When suddenly I got sucked into my phone.
I arrived in the world bit by bit,
Not knowing where to go or what to do.

A small, abandoned dog came to my feet,
It had cute, blinking electronic eyes and flappy ears.
The dog rolled over, begging for food
So I fed him screws and nails with my pair of pliers.

Two mysterious awards guarding the exits stopped
The dog, who I named Electro, ran after the two guards
I stepped into the portal and landed in my bed.

I suddenly awoke to the sound of the alarm,
I had to run downstairs to eat my breakfast
Goodbye phone and also my dog, Electro.

Torin De Silva (9)
Herington House School, Hutton Mount

An Adventure

I'm with my friends, going to the zoo
With animals coming out of the blue
When we arrive, to my surprise,
Monkeys are eating an assortment of pies.

We visit the anxious monkeys
Arguing with the dumb donkeys
Myself, Chloe, Izzy and Bruno Mars,
Are stuffing our faces with chocolate bars.

The zebras escape,
All rushing through the electric tape,
What's going to happen?
I think they are going to take action.

We search and search but with no luck,
We search for an hour but all we found was muck.
Suddenly, I awake with a jump
Falling off my bed with a tremendous thump.

Romy Skarott (9)
Herington House School, Hutton Mount

Once Upon A Dream

I was running in the field
A stick I did wield
The air had a strong breeze,
I felt like I was about to freeze.

It was cold and foggy,
And I was a bit soggy
Then there was a sudden whoosh,
It felt like a great big push.

It was a bird, a black, graceful swallow
Then it landed in a tree that was completely hollow.
It started to peck at some bird seed,
Then it looked up and stared at me.

Suddenly, it flew away
Then I thought I heard someone say,
'Wake up, wake up, it's almost lunch,
I think you need to have a munch.'

Harry Clarke (10)
Herington House School, Hutton Mount

The Forest

I can hear the howls from wolves
And the laughing of witches
I'm in a forest, creatures lie waiting,
They are big and sly, greedy and vicious,
Looking to find a tasty morsel.

Around me ghosts come out,
They are tall and small, vivid and colourless.
They will find me wherever I am,
They will take the spirit but leave the rest behind.

I wake up with sweat on my clothes,
Thank goodness it was a dream,
But I definitely won't go back there,
Or the wolves, witches, creatures and ghosts
Will be waiting just for me.

Dilan Kanagasabai (9)
Herington House School, Hutton Mount

Out In Space

As I stepped out into space,
I thought to myself, *What a mysterious place
to be!* There is a dream,
It looks like I'm watching a cinema screen.

When you're in space, there are billions of stars
I definitely can't see any cars
I'm looking at the Milky Way
And watching out for alien rays.

If you ever come out here,
And feel your heart is full of fear
Just remember what I said,
And you won't have any dread.

Harry Toms (9)
Herington House School, Hutton Mount

Once Upon A Dream!

I was running
The monster was cunning
Frost froze my hair
I didn't care
I stopped at a cliff
My legs went stiff
Then I was in bed
The sheets were red
I flicked on a light
It was ever so bright
My hair was tied up in a plait
My cat on the bed was taking a nap
I then got up quickly
My back felt prickly
As I stepped outside the bedroom door
I came face to face with a giant boar
'Where am I?' I murmured
'I do not know,' replied the boar
His voice was low
Then I noticed hanging around my neck
A sapphire heart filled with several black specks
Without thinking I raced down the stairs
I ran into a bundle of eight tiny bears
They nuzzled my hands in delight

I wasn't sure if they would bite
I stepped outdoors
There were no stores
There were no flats
There were no cats
There was no noise
Or any toys
In the distance
I saw a resistance
There were dragons pulling wagons
Giant horses jerking corpses
I rushed inside
To my surprise
The bears and boar were gone
My face turned long
I hurt my head
Then I went to bed
I crept under the sheets
I dreamed about sweets
Then I woke up.

Devon Charlotte Batho (11)
Ludwell Primary School, Ludwell

Yum, Yum Land

First I was drifting to sleep,
Then I thought of a dream,
It wasn't a game,
I had seen a unicorn that was made from cream.

The dream was in Yum Yum Land
That squishy, yummy, eatable chocolate house,
There was no law and no clean hands,
And my favourite McDonald's.

I went to my chocolate house,
I played on my not chocolate 3DS for an hour
Then I drank the chocolate from the chocolate fountain,
Then I went to not chocolate McDonald's
Then I ordered chips and a Mario toy.

I ate some McDonald's for free,
With colourful, cream unicorn
Then I found a tiny, small key,
Then I woke up when I touched the key,
So I never touched the key ever again.

Josh Dixon (9)
Northside Primary School, Northside

Day Scare

I slowly dozed off to bed,
A dream was coming up soon,
I slowly rested my head,
Then I thought I was at the moon.

I was with my happy mates,
Then I admired a huge swing,
Something was on the gates,
It was a weird, wacky thing.

I turned around, a 360 turn,
Then all of my friends were gone,
I thought I was going to burn,
All people, they were none.

The sun smiled with glee,
The trees slept with comfort,
It really cheered me,
The sky was lit by the sun.

But then I roughly fell down,
Ow! It really, really hurt
Oh no! It was a spooky clown,
His name must be Bert.
But then I woke up safe,
Safe and sound at home.

Finlay Tweedie (8)
Northside Primary School, Northside

The Super Dream

I didn't prepare for what was coming
I'm flying in the air like an eagle
And I thought I saw something running
It turns out it was just an eagle.

I flew back up in the air
I saw a golden Pegasus
Then there was a massive bear
Only to know it doesn't exist.

I'm flying along with squirrel girl.
Without knowing how I was flying
Then I did a twirl
Then I went shopping.

I was wearing a black and grey suit,
With a 'B' in the middle
Then there was a big host
Then I saw Lidl.

I woke up to see it was just a dream
Everything is solved
Then I let out a big scream
Then my mum called.

Ryan Fell (9)
Northside Primary School, Northside

Papa Bear

I was galloping through a river,
On a big, brown horse called Quiver,
I had a frightening scare,
Oh no, it was a papa bear.

That papa bear had a mare,
Should I dare go over there?
But I did, 'cause that was my job,
When I got there, it looked like my boss, Bob.

I can see trees dancing,
I can see baby lambs prancing,
I can hear the wind singing a song,
I see a green snake about ten feet long.

Finally, I opened my eyes
To find out I had a surprise,
I had a look, it was my dream book,
There I was, standing on the bear's book.

Madison Pickering (9)
Northside Primary School, Northside

Fright Night

I was in hospital, a scary one too,
An old man yelled at me, boo!
The foot kicked a ball,
A tall zombie made me fall.

Quickly I stood up tall,
I dropped the crisps from the mall,
Like a bear it gave me a scare,
I ran like I didn't care.

The sky was angry with lightning,
It was very frightening,
It cracked a grave,
There was the zombie wave.

I got a gigantic surprise,
My big old brother said 'rise,'
I open my eyes,
I never got to say my goodbyes.

Thomas James Busby (9)
Northside Primary School, Northside

The Nasty Clown

I was in a creepy forest,
I saw a nasty clown,
I ran away but it was too fast,
Oh no! I tumbled down.

I was very terrified,
I tried to call for help,
I tried to reach in my pocket,
Oh no! My phone battery was dead.

I saw a terrifying cave,
Creepy, dark and damp,
I quietly went in the cave,
It was full of weapons and a lamp.

I got caught by the clown,
I ran away from the clown!

Was it just a dream?

Aidan Lee Sharp (9)
Northside Primary School, Northside

The Stadium

I rapidly ran away to sleep
Then I had a little peep,
I opened my eyes and saw my stadium,
Then I met my friend called Damien.

After a while I went to the tunnel,
Where I saw a magic funnel,
So I picked it up and gave it to Naldo,
Then the crowd shouted, 'Ronaldo!'

Then I scored a beautiful goal,
But there was a little mole
Then it said it had a bed,
But it sounded like my friend, Ted.

Levi Earl (9)
Northside Primary School, Northside

Untitled

I ran into the forest to see the unicorn,
And then I ran into a magical tree,
Because I was too excited,
And then I saw a bright eye,
It was a unicorn
It was beautiful.

Sonny Coulson (7)
Northside Primary School, Northside

All Our Precious Dreams

All our precious dreams are full of hope and wonder,
Dreams of rainbows and maybe, sometimes of thunder,
We dream of unicorns and dancing bears,
And maybe even people with funny hairs,
We can dream of animals that can talk,
And mysterious ghosts that always stalk.

Dreams of you being famous,
Exactly like Tori Amos,
We dream of us having superpowers,
And helping people for hours and hours,
All our precious dreams are full of hope and wonder,
Dreams of rainbows and maybe, sometimes of thunder.

Dreams of an abandoned forest creeping you out,
And also a monster who's making you shout,
We dream of a world with sweets and candyfloss
And also bring with the Wizard of Oz,
All our precious dreams are full of hope and wonder,
Dreams of rainbows and maybe, sometimes of thunder.

Divina Sivajoti (10)
SS Peter & Paul RC Primary School, Redland

Time For Bed!

'Time for bed,' Mum calls, 'and hurry up!'
I can't - it's far too early!
Do you really expect me
To sleep at 9.30pm?

'Get to bed and I mean now!'
So reluctantly, I don't know how,
I brush my teeth and get to bed,
Thoughts and fears prowl in my head.

I won't go to sleep,
I'm not even tired!
But maybe when I do drop off
The nightmare will have left my mind?

I'm struggling now, trying not to count sheep,
But I'm so tired,
One or two minutes of sleep?

No. No, I've only gone and done it!
It's all black around me,
And down, down I plummet.

I fall to the ground and look left and right,
And as I look over my shoulder,
I get a huge fright!

It isn't... it can't be..
Oh no, it is...
Mr Moky!

The meanest teacher in our school
Strode up beside me.
He was carrying piles of paper.
'These are for you,' says he.

I look up at the towering mound,
Every topic is here!
I can't do this - I'll never finish!
This is my greatest fear.

Katie Skiffington (10)
SS Peter & Paul RC Primary School, Redland

The Imaginary Bicycle Race

I woke up in a bicycle race,
But I had no vehicle,
Although I wasn't at their pace,
I chased the bicycle race!

As I was running,
I saw the riders riding,
It was Vincent van Gogh,
But then he fell off.

So, sneakily I hitched a ride,
I rode Vincent van Gogh's bike with pride!

Then I rammed Cressida Cowel,
Who was wearing a towel,
She spoke some dragonese,
'Could you move to the left, please?'

As soon as I overtook Cressida,
I met Zoe in her boat called Lucy,
She came from an island called Norwich,
Which in *Floodland* is now a ditch?

I could name all the authors and artists in that race,
But at a very slow pace,
I ended up first and had met all the authors, artists and characters,
Thanks for reviewing my dream, full of hopes and wonders.

James Taylor (9)
SS Peter & Paul RC Primary School, Redland

My Dreams

In a dream I can do what I want to do
See what I want to see
And hear what I want to hear
Because it is my unique dream
Mine to keep forever and ever.

I've been everywhere in my dreams
Spectrum HQ,
Diagon Alley,
And even Deep Dean School for Girls with its murderous headmistress.

Sometimes nightmares come and go
One second you're having the time of your life
And the next, shadows of the witch, dragon, vampire or snake loom in,
In they creep, the horrible things
And the joy turns into fear.

But the dreams I like to have the most
Are to imagine the adventures I might go on
So plant the seeds of your future,
Go on, do it, I dare you,
And make your dreams happen.
It is your chance to see what the future could hold.

Francesca Harvey (11)
SS Peter & Paul RC Primary School, Redland

My Little Dream

When I'm older, I want to dance
I want to send the audience into a trance
Four years ago, I danced on May Day
My tutu could be seen from miles away.

But when I go to sleep, it's different in the night
Suddenly my ballet dream starts to take flight
I go to a costume room to get my white tutu and get dressed
I must look my absolute best.

I dance Swan Lake for all my fans
Suddenly, I hear them clap their hands.

Twenty years later, my dream came true
Just like my mother always knew
This could never have happened without my dream.
At least that is how it seems,
I'm a ballerina for all to see,
This is who I want to be.

Now that I professionally dance,
I like to send my audience into a trance.

Lily Loughlin (10)
SS Peter & Paul RC Primary School, Redland

My Lands In The Sky

I dream of magical lands in the sky,
Where all creatures can talk, where I can fly.
In my dreams I visit many places,
Of dragons and hydras with many, many faces.

I let my happiest thoughts run wild,
Luring something to my face - a smile.
In my wonderful world made on dreams,
Anything can happen, it may seem.

In my undiscovered world far, far away,
I fight dragons and cast spells all in one day.
With streams of excitement in the North, South, East and West,
This everlasting land is truly the best.

My marvellous journey does come to an end,
And I do leave my creatures, (best, best, best friends).
But what gets me through it, is knowing there's more,
There is only one problem, I don't know what's in store.

Iris Taylor (10)
SS Peter & Paul RC Primary School, Redland

How Dreams Began

At the core of the Earth,
Was the place where dreams gave birth,
Dreams in jars, high and low,
They were put there forever and not allowed to go.

Dreams of astronauts, spiders and clowns,
Bad dreams so grumpy they always had a frown,
And dreams of sparking writers,
Famous fairies and dashing young firefighters.
Once dreams had finished their time,
The dreams sought eager, hungry minds,
Each day by day, they made new finds.

Thud! Crack!
A meteor hit,
Shelves banged the ground with a *thwack!*
The jars shattered into tiny bits,
The dreams had been set free,
Not knowing what they were doing,
Glistening dreams floated up and around thee,
And dreams these days are still achieving, still pursuing.

Rivie Tilly Bates
SS Peter & Paul RC Primary School, Redland

My Loving Fairy

Oh what a lovely dream,
My dreams that I had yesterday,
About my guardian fairy,
The only place where I see her is in my lovely dream.

My dream is filled with stars
But between all those stars
Appears my guardian fairy
Small and beautiful like all of them.

She talks to me and calls me by my name,
She says that she is there,
To help me to make my dreams come true
She will always be there when I will need her.

Then suddenly my dream was ending,
And my eyes were opening,
I realised that my guardian fairy was someone I loved
And had by my side every day.

Oh dear Mother,
You, my guardian fairy, will forever be,
I am happy because I have you
And I always want to love you.

Geraldine Cross Rosales (10)
SS Peter & Paul RC Primary School, Redland

Once Upon A...

Snug in my bed,
After I've read,
I dream whilst asleep,
Until the alarm goes *beep!*

Harry Potter's in my dreams,
Quite a lot, or so it seems,
Sometimes Voldemort appears,
He is one of my greatest fears.

In my dreams, I can go anywhere,
I've even hunted for a bear,
Swishing, swashing through the grass,
On a school trip with my class.

Miss Grayling led us, strict but fair,
We girls were dashing here and there,
Trekking through the stormy showers,
We longed to be back at Malory Towers.

I wonder if you've figured out,
What my dreams are all about?
I've tried to give you lots of help,
You'll find my dreams upon my shelf.

Katie Anna Watts (9)
SS Peter & Paul RC Primary School, Redland

Eleanor's Dream Gift

Yes, yes, it's Eleanor's birthday
She's having a disco, let's get ready to party!

Oh no, I don't have a gift,
No worries, I'll go to the shops and buy something swift.

What's this? She wants no presents?
She's decided to give money to charity.
That's amazing because I can definitely say
That's not for me, I need some clarity!

I ask her why, she says, 'To buy is too much
I have a house full of stuff, I'm happy,
Best I give money to a good cause!'

She's amazing, she's great, go Eleanor, she's my mate!
It's my birthday soon, I'm thinking of gifts
But maybe a charity won't go a miss.

Fergus McDonald (10)
SS Peter & Paul RC Primary School, Redland

Dreams

A dream is something late at night
A dream is something at early dawn,
A dream is something that ebbs away
And sometimes it lingers for another day.

I dreamt of Harry Potter
And his wonderful wizarding ways,
I dreamt of going to platform nine and three quarters,
Abracadabra!
And it did totally amaze.

Feeling like the number one,
Racing round the city,
Having ups and downs,
And all around
Zooming up the highest mounds
My nightmare has snuck back again.

My happy thoughts are gone,
Waking up with a big loud scream,
Thank goodness, it was just a dream!

Harry Harvey (9)
SS Peter & Paul RC Primary School, Redland

A Land Of Equality

I have a dream
A land of peace and joy
Equality rights,
For every girl and boy.

No one judges you,
On your religion or race,
Or how many scars
And spots on your face.

They judge you
On who you are on the inside
They respect your differences
So there's nothing to hide.

It doesn't matter
Whether you are woman or man,
Or whether you're disabled,
No one says you can't or you can.

I have a dream
People judge you on personality,
Everyone with freedom and rights,
A land of equality.

Lara Smith (10)
SS Peter & Paul RC Primary School, Redland

Dreams

Where will your imagination take you?

I dreamed of being brave and bold,
Fighting monster from years of old
Who cursed me with freezing cold
And not doing what I was told?

Where will your imagination take you?

I dreamed of being really shy
And having kittens by my side
However, in public I start to cry
Then I start to run in fear and hide.

Where will your imagination take you?

The land of dreaming is a magical place
There is no limit, not even the sky

What will your imagination make you?

Theodore Bradwell (9)
SS Peter & Paul RC Primary School, Redland

Football On The Moon

F ootball on the dusty moon is my special dream
O ut on the pitch which is dark and dusty like meteors have hit
O utside on the huge moon we start to float around in the gigantic stadium
T oday the golden ball bounces in the dark sky at night
B lack as coal, we still played onwards
A t this moment, I realised the unbelievable crowd wore red and black shirts
L ater I found out that I was in the team for the cup final
L ate in the game, I scored five goals, my team were overjoyed when they were crowned champions of the dream world cup 2027!

Noah Scott (10)
SS Peter & Paul RC Primary School, Redland

The Mysterious Island

When I sailed through the sea in my trusty boat,
I see an island covered in fog,
Terrified, I tried to sail away
But I just got pulled in.

As soon as I got onto the island,
I was attacked by bloodthirsty natives,
Until there was a roar,
I was in grave danger.

Exploring was difficult,
I pretty much almost died straight away
With that giant ape almost squishing me,
And getting attacked by giant bugs.

I climbed out carefully,
But then I fell right back in,
Suddenly I woke up
To find that it was a dream!

Ryan Agenonga Prince Kanua (10)
SS Peter & Paul RC Primary School, Redland

Poem To My Book

Once upon a dream where I write my dear book
I am here sat on front of my desk on my house of the mountain
I write you based on the sea waves of a beach.
I write you accompanied by my family.
I write you inspired, happy and creative.
I draw mythical creatures and fantasies over you.
I write you, I publish you and I win my first prize.
My prize inspires me to write my second book.
You, my second book, will create consciousness about global warming
I don't know if you will make me win a prize
I will write you with creativity and passion, my dream book!

Dylan Romero (10)
SS Peter & Paul RC Primary School, Redland

Amazing Space

When I look up in the sky, I dream that I am in space.
Whizzing through the Milky Way and visiting all the planets not yet discovered,
Discovering aliens who people don't believe in
When I look up at the sky, I dream that I'm in space
Riding a rocket through the unknown bits of space,
When I look out the window, I see the brightly shining stars
Which makes me think I'm in outer space
Which looks like it's one million eyes constantly watching.
The moon is a huge eye which always watches me.
Space is amazing, it's a dream come true!

Aswin Jayan (9)
SS Peter & Paul RC Primary School, Redland

Recipe For A Dream

Firstly, boil dream water
After, add a pinch of imagination
Stir until nice and pink
After, get a tablespoon of sleeping powder
Put that in another bowl
After, take some magic think bubbles.
Put them in the mixture of sleeping powder,
Take your bowl of dream water and imagination
Add your sleeping powder and think bubbles in it
After, mix until nice and thick so you can shape it
Put the thick mixture in a tray
Bake until it is colourful like a rainbow.

After, eat it with happiness and...
Have sweet dreams!

Ann Siby Stephen (10)
SS Peter & Paul RC Primary School, Redland

My Pet Dragon

I've got my pet dragon, nice and close to me,
When I go to bed, I set my dragon free.

My dragon breathes fire, my dragon breathes ice,
In my amazing dreams, he seems really nice.

He has scaly skin and really sharp teeth,
He's very, very tough and his name is Keith.

My dragons likes to fly high up in the sky,
When he wants to eat, I dream him up a pie.

I've got my pet dragon curled up on my head,
I'll set him free tomorrow when I'm tucked up in bed.

Oliver Clayton (9)
SS Peter & Paul RC Primary School, Redland

Dreaming Of Dreams!

Lying on the beach,
Having fun,
Dreaming of whales,
Splashing their tails.

Oh what a sight,
I can't wait.
For tonight,
What it would be like.

In my dream,
My never-ending dream,
I never knew,
What I thought I could be.

A fairy, a pirate,
Anything you want,
You name it,
It is there.

I love my dreams,
I don't want them to end,
'Cause they're just for me and you,
'Til the very end.

Kejti Dushaj (10)
SS Peter & Paul RC Primary School, Redland

Nightmare

N othing comes near the night, only darkness
I hate the dark, only light will light me up to shine the day
G ood days always light me up to give ways through the dark paths.
H ow did darkness go through light when it was scary and bright?
T errified, I lie here in my bed waiting for
M orning to come and save me.
A ll around me there are freaky noises that make me
R un away from my dreams and
E scape to my parents' bed.

Serena Alexandra Williams López (8)
SS Peter & Paul RC Primary School, Redland

Monsters!

As I climb in my bed,
I see in my head,
The mysteries that appear,
And also make me fear.

The monsters in the night,
Give me quite a fright,
But I know deep inside,
They have a bright light.

As I climb on your back,
You let me have a nap.
I feel your prickly spikes
Crawl on my spine.

Now it's time to go,
I need to let you know.
I'll come back next week,
When I go back to sleep.

Lola Cortes Hyland (9)
SS Peter & Paul RC Primary School, Redland

Magical Land

I discovered an old oak tree
I looked closely and there I saw
A beautifully carved wooden door
Through the door I went
And what a sight I saw!
Trees full of summer fruit tasting sweets
Stunning flowers that sprout lemonade
Oh, what a treat!
A pond glimmering with fairy dust
This amazing land is my secret
You must trust
I'll come back again some day
When my dream takes me this way.

Edie Jeans (8)
SS Peter & Paul RC Primary School, Redland

Pirate Adventure

Sailing the seven seas,
With my pirate shipmates,
Scaring my enemies,
Because I'm Blackbeard the Fierce.

Celebrating victories,
Searching for merchant ships,
Making them walk the plank,
Because I'm Blackbeard the Fierce.

Trying to find treasure,
Finding glorious maps,
I love to dig up gold,
Because I'm Blackbeard the Fierce.

Kevin Jerome (10)
SS Peter & Paul RC Primary School, Redland

Dreams

A dream can take
You far away
To mystical lands
Right now, today.

All you have to do
Is close your eyes
And let go of the
Things that you despise.

I had a dream
Of times to come
A time of peace
With lots of fun.

If you have a dream
To believe in too
I would recommend it
Through and through.

Maeva Page Cotton (10)
SS Peter & Paul RC Primary School, Redland

Dreams

D reams, dreams are full of things
R ethink in the blink of an eye
E veryone you will remember and love
A mazing things you will think about
M emories come flooding in
S weetness is filled inside them from the front to the back.

I love dreams to the moon and back.

Olivia Downie (8)
SS Peter & Paul RC Primary School, Redland

When I Lose You

Without you I feel pain
You hurt me,
But you don't mean any harm.

We called each other names,
But we didn't mean to
When I lost you, I lost something in my heart.

I hope this isn't meant to end this way
But I know soon we'll forgive and forget.

Antonia Garcia (9)
SS Peter & Paul RC Primary School, Redland

How To Make A Dream

First add a pinch of passion,
Then spray dream water,
After, throw in a bunch of thought bubbles
Then a sprinkle of imaginations,
Pour in bits of daydreams,
Stir it with sleep powder,
And then add happy juice
Spray creative water,
Finally, put it in an oven of dream.

Steve Siby Stephen (10)
SS Peter & Paul RC Primary School, Redland

Mr Space Pig

Yesterday afternoon,
I had a dream
I flew to the moon
On a pig.

His name was Mr Space Pig,
Short for Stig,
It was lovely until I went to sleep.

All my dreams were still there
Oh how lovely, it was there
Now Stig is always in my head.

Anthony Shedov (10)
SS Peter & Paul RC Primary School, Redland

Dream

D aring adventures of pirates and mermaids
R are creatures like unicorns and dragons
E nchanting smelly underpants
A nd foxes with wings
M y dream is my dream.

Bea Blackman (9)
SS Peter & Paul RC Primary School, Redland

What Lurks Under My Bed

I fluff my pillow and jump into my bed
I lay down and rest my head.

Mum turns out the light and wishes me goodnight
Then the nightmares begin.
I tell my shaking body that there are:
No ghosts or ghouls.
No witches nor worms.
No bats or dragons nor megalodons.
No spider that creeps.
Or monstrous jelly heaps.
No skeletons or dinosaurs
Or even Minotaurs.

There are no monsters under my bed
My head is securely tucked under my duvet
My head is dripping with body sweat from my shaking worry.
I slide my eyelids open to see if anything stirs
Then I hear an odd murmur
The duvet peels off my body from my gluey sweat
My bed gives a jerk then something must lurk
Something has to linger, will they chop off my finger?
I let out a yelp and shout for help, but it's only my parents back from work.

Bethan Daly (10)
St Vigor & St John CE Primary School, Chilcompton

Last Night I Dreamed

Last night I dreamed
Of autumn
A cascade of multicoloured leaves
Spiralling down
A blaze of glory.

Last night I dreamed
Of winter
An endless white wonderland
In all its glory
A relentless snowstorm.

Last night I dreamed
Of spring
Flowers bloom
A circle of colour
As the animals return.

Last night I dreamed
Of summer
The temperatures rising
The sun blazing down on the Earth
As the nights turn from dark to bright.

Last night I dreamed
Of nightmarish creatures
The jaws that rip
The claws that catch
As I drift away.

Last night I dreamed
Of the wildlife
Struggling for survival
The seas rising
The ice melting.

Last night I dreamed
Of the stars
A bright light to follow
Leading to a new world
And then going away in a supernova.

Last night I dreamed
Of wolves
Howling through the night
The moon shines down on them
Like a diamond.

Jamie White (10)
St Vigor & St John CE Primary School, Chilcompton

Double Dream

I ran down the never-ending hallway
In sight, I see crimson red eyes
Getting bigger and bigger
As I stood, the eyes started glowing more and more.
I was stuck - like I'm in quicksand.
I tried to cower in the corner in the dark
But the eyes got closer and closer
Now I saw a dagger - like teeth grinning with a smile so menacing, I got goosebumps
Then it said, 'Wakey, wakey, rise and shine.'
I woke, it was just my mum.

But did she always have her hair red?
'Oh no, I'm in another dream,' I said in dread.
The clock on my wall was spinning like crazy,
Everything was feeling a tiny bit hazy,
I was feeling ever so lazy,
I wanted to wake up,
Suddenly everything disappeared and I was in my room
But wait, am I still asleep?

Luke Mitchelmore (10)
St Vigor & St John CE Primary School, Chilcompton

Lost In The Woods

'Charlie, Noah, where are you guys?'
I'm all alone in the woods, and it's dark,
There is very little light and the trees seem to be getting closer.
The shadows are like people coming to get me.
I start to run, but I don't know where I am going.
What's that noise?
Is it one of my friends?
There's no one there, only the trees.
The trees are getting closer and they are surrounding me.
I'm petrified!
I don't know where to go.
What should I do?
What was that?
I heard a voice, someone's shouting my name.
I can hear Noah, he is getting closer.
I shout back, there he is again.
I see him, he is coming towards me.
But where is Charlie?
I think he is lost in the woods.

Matt Denning Maggs (10)
St Vigor & St John CE Primary School, Chilcompton

The Dread Of The Haunted Castle

In the blackness I stood,
Lonely and cold.
Wispy figures surrounded me.
Their ancient faces stared.
It felt like a bullet was going through me,
I shivered.
As I tiptoed up the stairs,
The figures followed.
A sense of panic shot through me.
I sprinted up the stairs,
Gasping for breath,
I dashed into the closest room to me.

The ghosts soon found me.
One spread a wicked grin,
I took a step back.
The floor started to shake,
A hole appeared and I fell into it,
I closed my eyes.
The hole was like an endless portal.
Suddenly I awoke,
I was staring at the ceiling,
Thank goodness it was just a dream!

Keira Maundrill (10)
St Vigor & St John CE Primary School, Chilcompton

My Dream

In the night, we all have dreams
But we can't always remember them
But this dream stands out over all the rest
Do you know why? No... Well you'll just find out
It was just a splendiferous dream!
There were birds and people and monsters and flying
This dream will be famous.

Just imagine this:
Your best friend's a raccoon
Your teacher is a baboon
Your daddy, he's a loon,
Let's bust a gumball goon
You're in a band that's out of tune
You're sleeping in a comfy cocoon
They look all dried up like prunes
Imagine that. It's hard to believe, isn't it?

Drew Reuben Box (11)
St Vigor & St John CE Primary School, Chilcompton

The Piano

The low notes fire at me like bullets,
The music surrounds me,
It rings constantly in my numb ears,
I begin to float, raising higher and higher until I reach the clouds
The music gets rapidly louder again.

'Help me, piano, help me escape,' I say.
Keys start to gather around me
The deeper and darker notes hit hard at their chests
Creating a ferocious wave of sound,
The high notes begin too and I'm suddenly falling,
How can this dream turn into a nightmare?
How can you do this to me, head?
I finally pinch myself and find that I am safely tucked under the sheets of my nice, warm bed.

Izzy (10)
St Vigor & St John CE Primary School, Chilcompton

Audience Piano Time

One night I was in bed
I went downstairs and flew to the moon,
I didn't know what was happening until,
I saw my best friend Izzy up in the magical sky,
Then I spotted my Nan, so easy to see.

In the corner of my eye, I saw my Mum flying to me
We all had a dream of performing in front of a crowd
But we know that wouldn't happen ever.

I saw pink clouds, that wasn't right
I saw lollipops waiting to be licked
I saw rainbows that I could touch
I love chocolate
I love chocolate drops
I hate rain
I hate raindrops.

Leah (10)
St Vigor & St John CE Primary School, Chilcompton

Football Boys

F orever I will love my football
O nly if I believe in myself I will become a footballer
O ver in the Etihad stadium is where I belong
T oday I will become my dream
B ehind me is hope waiting to become real to me
A ll of my fans believe in me
L ove is everywhere
L ife you can't change.

B eyond my dreams is another football team
O verall, football is the best
Y ou can become anything in your dream
S ome hope is lurking around me and everyone else on Earth.

Oliver Tibbs (10)
St Vigor & St John CE Primary School, Chilcompton

Asleep

You wake in a room, still in bed,
But this isn't your room, why are the walls red?
You see a hole as big as a frying pan, no wider
Out jumps a thing onto your head, oh no, it's a spider!
Asleep, you look down from a window at three oddly dressed men,
One had a label stating he is called Ken,
They hid in a log next to a wall,
Many more men come and one starts to call,
'No people here,' he said to Paul
You awake from just a dream without hearing the faint pitter-patter of eight legs.

Noah Godber (11)
St Vigor & St John CE Primary School, Chilcompton

The Rabbit Hole

As me and my friends walk along,
We come across a rabbit hole,
My friends dared but I do not,
With fear of never getting out.

We walked towards the dreaded place,
Ella with pride and Lara with bravery,
And I was full of fear,
They both jumped down the rabbit hole as I backed away.

My friends come back safe and sound, showing no regret,
My fear transformed to courage, leading me to the hole,
I jumped right down, slipped through and never came back.

Sofia Amelie Todd (11)
St Vigor & St John CE Primary School, Chilcompton

The Magic Of Imagination

Imagination,
It creates a whole world,
Where the brain runs wild,
Full of thoughts, good and bad
Nothing is complete if it's not there.

Imagination,
What would we do without it?
Everything comes from imagination,
The tallest tower to the smallest brick,
Someone thinks it
And it becomes real.

Imagination
It fuels the mind, causing it to expand
Making way for more creative thoughts to come
This is the magic of imagination.

James Peter Rideout (10)
St Vigor & St John CE Primary School, Chilcompton

Monochrome

I drop off to sleep after a dreary day,
I can't get to sleep, what's in my way?
I get to sleep, white powder envelopes me
I get up, I hear a voice, it's a she.

'Seb, thank goodness it's you.'
It's a girl from school but she's only new
A billowing white cloud appears on the horizon,
I can't see her, but her voice's pitch is rising.

'Help!' I run to save her
But I trip
I'm falling, falling...

Sebestyén Ciprián Tahin (10)
St Vigor & St John CE Primary School, Chilcompton

Mrs Fairy

Oh, Mrs Fairy
Where were you last night?
I waited by your house to hug you goodnight.

I looked everywhere for you
But I did not see your sparkly wand
Or your pretty dress
Instead I got lost, I was getting in a mess.

I heard lots of noises
Which gave me quite a fright
I woke up straight away to realise
You were not in sight.

Anyway, Mrs Fairy, when will I see you next?
I hope it's tonight in my warm, comfy bed.

Grace May Pritchard (11)
St Vigor & St John CE Primary School, Chilcompton

Winners!

W inning the match would be a dream come true,
I n a stadium where famous players have played, now me too.
N earing the end of the match, only two minutes to go, I smash the ball with all my might,
N earing the top right-hand corner, a goal for me in the back
E xciting the stadium, a hero to the crowd.
R oaring, we have done it.
S inging as we came, 'Hallelujah, hallelujah, we are the champions, we've won the Premier League.'

Ben Taylor (11)
St Vigor & St John CE Primary School, Chilcompton

Nature's Journey

The glimmering water swayed,
Surrounded by a cluster of trees
The air swirled delicately
Lifting the fragile sand,
As the sun glares down.

The water's tide splashes in rage,
The trees topple down, engulfing themselves into the ground,
The ferocious air rapidly rushes,
The sand is lifted in the storm-like conditions scattering,
As the sun glares down almost blinding anyone who trespasses.

A boy,
A boat,
Obliterated.

Finley Button (10)
St Vigor & St John CE Primary School, Chilcompton

A Loyal Friend

When there's tears rolling down your face
I'll be there, in the same place
When you call my name, it'll all be the same
I'll be there, always in arm's reach
When it's your time to shine
My loving eyes will look upon you
I know we will make it through
But if there ever comes a day when we can't be together
Keep me in your heart
And let my spirit protect you forever
Forever loved
Forever loyal
I am the dog.

Amber C Rayner (11)
St Vigor & St John CE Primary School, Chilcompton

Not This Time

In a blind panic,
Racing through the wood
Ominous breathing behind,
Laughing yellow cat eyes give chase,
Terrifying trauma gushing blood,
Trees trap and whip
Fog falling
Cliff ahead
End of the line
Not this time
I turn
Crossbow in hand
Silver tipped arrow in the moonlight
The tables have turned
Now who's scared?
The arrow released
It's time for the beast
To flee and let me rest in peace.

Finley Lachlan Hunter-Clarke (10)
St Vigor & St John CE Primary School, Chilcompton

Scream And Shout

The lights, the pitch, the whole stadium lit up
I heard the crowd roaring my name
The tunnel was pitch black.

The bright green grass felt as soft as pillows
The other red and black team lined up
We stomped over, not letting the other team see we were fearless
The other team did the same.

We shook hands firmly, smiling
As we ran to our places, the crowd stopped
The whistle blew, the game had begun.

Toby Jones (11)
St Vigor & St John CE Primary School, Chilcompton

The Great Fight Of the Pirates

The sea was sploshing on their boat
Swords were clashing while they float,
Some are dead without their head,
Some are alive, will they survive?
Some shall survive, many shall die,
Gunshots were fired
Swords were swung.

Two are alive, who shall survive?
Swords are down, guns are up,
One shot was fired, a life was expired.

I woke up in my comfy bed
I was so glad I still had my head.

Holly Devlin (10)
St Vigor & St John CE Primary School, Chilcompton

Skeleton

Being chased around by a skeleton,
Leaving blood everywhere from its bones,
Offering to have food.
Dying for food
Ending its life from no food,
Dehydrated from no water.

Seeing its skinny bone coming from round the corner,
Crunching its teeth on skin,
Ending up trapped,
Leaving the skeleton to come into view
The skeleton eats onto my skin
Never opening my eyes again.

Calvin Glover (11)
St Vigor & St John CE Primary School, Chilcompton

The Bunny Nightmare

Around me all I see is the dark
Then suddenly a pair of green eyes
I try to scream but no sound comes out
Not knowing where I'm going, I feel something sharp
My heart is jumping up and down
The injection bunny!
My fear is realised
I run, I run for my life
Then I fall to the floor
And I know my bed is too small!

Dominika Eliza Kudyba (11)
St Vigor & St John CE Primary School, Chilcompton

Burn

A licking tongue of death and heat,
Ever pursuing,
Ever consuming,
Infectious and spreading from log to log,
Scolding and hungry
Forever eating, and forever hunting
Inescapable yet beautiful,
Rising up into the sky and burning the clouds.

Oliver Grace (11)
St Vigor & St John CE Primary School, Chilcompton

Beating Up The Base

B eing around music can make people happy.
E nding with a bad tune, can make the song scrappy.
A iring up the base, make sure you keep up with the pace.
T he music can be very loud
I n the puffy clouds
N ote-taking can be good
G oing out with the hood.

U ncontrollable dancing
P uffing up with prancing.

T he music makes you start bopping
H ungry and sopping
E asy-going tunes.

B opping in the middle of June
A bove all cried out that little pound.
S lowly, around the theatre all the way round
E nter the music hood!

Georgi O'Neill (11)
Whybridge Junior School, Rainham

My Bestie And The Beast

Lauren is my best friend
We're together more than it seems,
Even when I sleep at night,
She joins me in my dreams!

We were having a little stroll,
In-between the trees,
We turned the corner,
Oh! A haunted house we see!

We passed the gate,
It creaked as it closed
We looked up at the sky
And the moon began to glow.

We walked up the steps that led to the door,
We shut it behind us,
And investigated some more.

I looked at Lauren,
Lauren looked at me,
We were both scared,
As possible as can be!

We heard a noise,
We heard a creak,

We turned around
To see the big, bad beast!

Lauren screamed,
I screamed too,
We held each other's hand
Because that's what best friends do.

We ran to the door
As quick as we could
We turned for a second,
To see where we stood.

Running through the forest,
Back towards the gate,
We got stuck in some mud
Unable to escape.

Hannah Pooley (10)
Whybridge Junior School, Rainham

Imagination

I dream so happily in my imagination with my mum.
M eeting new fairies which are so beautiful.
A nd the famous unicorn with a fluffy tail.
G laring left and right all I can see is fairies in a fright.
I meet a legendary wizard, he was evil.
N othing makes the fairies scared but the wizard.
A nd there was an angry fairy, very angry.
T hey want me to stay but I have to go, 'Bye bye' I say.
I run up the street and say bye to the wonderful fairy.
O ne day her father asked, 'Where have you and your mother been?'
N ever go without my permission, they all lived happily ever after.

Sara Abdi Hassan Mahmuud (8)
Whybridge Junior School, Rainham

Dance With Your Heart

Feel the force of nature as they pierce in your skin
Spin the world as the magic sinks in
Dance with your heart as you feel the wonder
Dance with your heart as it makes you want to ponder
The moon shone bright into my pupil eye,
I felt so happy, it made me want to cry.
It made me feel like a butterfly,
Who has just grown wings and is flying high,
It makes me want to move my body, even my thighs
As I moved, the touch of the grass
Felt as ripe as an apple
The tranquil breeze ruffled moonlight, scattered leaves.
I danced free, everyone was proud of me.
I danced with a beam
Oh! I remember, it was just a dream.

Mariam Nuhu (11)
Whybridge Junior School, Rainham

My Little Star!

Little star,
Little star,
Oh how bright that you are
You swing left to right
Up and down
You never stop to take
A breath
Twinkle, twinkle
Little star
Oh how bright
That you are
Count me once,
Count me twice
Twinke, twinkle
Little star.

When you see me high,
Up in the night sky you will feel,
A little light in your tummy.
Little star,
Little star,
Oh how bright that you are
You swing left to right,
Up and down,

You never stop to take
A breath
Twinkle, twinkle
Little star
Oh how bright
That you are
Twinkle, twinkle
Little star.

Lauren Hazell Daisey Patricia Hazell (10)
Whybridge Junior School, Rainham

Terrible Teachers!

Terrible teachers, that's all I see.
Around me, near me, that's where they'll be,
They can never find their spaces,
Always close to me,
I wish that they were toothless so I could have peace.

If only I moved schools, no stress will be near me,
Terrible teachers, annoying teachers
Why can't they go away, I see them every day.

Alone, alone, that's what I am,
Feeling left out, surrounded by bullies
I hate my school, I hate my house
Terrible teachers take over my life!

Why does this happen to me,
I wish I could be treated nicer,
But I am so unlucky!

Elizabeth Durojaiye (8)
Whybridge Junior School, Rainham

Forest Wildness

F orests are simple, my ones are different
O n top of the orange trees, I can see blue monkeys
R ivers filled with orange juice... mmm!
E la the elephant loves orange leaves!
S ensitive snakes, too scared to fight!
T alented monkeys, juggling coconuts!

W ater, water, where are you water?
I n the forest's palace we will sit
L ia the leopard covered with spots
D id it work or did it fail?
N ever fear, your forest saver is here!
E mma helps herself to the leaves
S illy little thing
S o laugh!

Nabila Hussain (9)
Whybridge Junior School, Rainham

Candy Land And The Sweet Witch

There was a time in Candy Land,
When the streets were bursting with treats,
With gingerbread houses,
Jelly bean trees and lollipop lights,
People were happy and full of delight.

Until such a day when along came a witch
Whose name just happened to be Mandy,
She was sneaky and horrible and stole all of the candy,
People were sad and all in a tizz
Oh where is the delicious candy?

In swooped the Barnys and captured the witch,
They found all the candy hidden in a ditch
They grabbed all the sweets
And returned all the treats
To make the people happy again.

Chloé Barnard (8)
Whybridge Junior School, Rainham

My Fairy Dream

M y wings are sparkling in the sun
Y es, I'm flying, this is fun.

F airy treehouses all made of wood
A mazing tiny places, wow this is so good
I find my other fairy friends
R uling their castle and setting new trends
Y ou might think my dream is amazing and cool.

D ay turns to night and here comes the storm
R ivers flowing fierce and wild
E xtreme weather ruins our smiles
A nastasia uses her magical powers
M agnificent fairy dust stops all rain and showers.

Mia Castello (9)
Whybridge Junior School, Rainham

Fairies! Oh No, We're Trapped!

There were three little girls running with glee,
As they wanted lots of tea
Their names were Mia, Annise and Zangi,
On their way home from school,
As adventurous as can be!

Tea was finished,
Earlier than usual,
How upsetting,
That the girls were fretting,
That they'd be going to bed early...

Bedtime, bedtime!
Awake as an eagle, started giggling at a naughty plan
Up to mischief, I'm not surprised
Huh! Caught by fairies!
This isn't real,
And locked up in a cage, in such a rage...

Annise Callender (9)
Whybridge Junior School, Rainham

A Splash Of Magic

Wizard, wizard, wizard, do some spells
Which are as colourful as the ocean shells.

Please, wizard, do some spells, we all want
To see the magic, ask all the world.

Finally, wizard you did some spells
Now we have to thank you for doing your wonderful
and magical spells.

Bye bye, wizard,
You can go now to your magical land that has never
been found.

Bye bye wizard, you have now gone,
Everyone will remember you as you have gone,
Now you are at home, you can sit on your magical
flying bed.

Jake Jackson (10)
Whybridge Junior School, Rainham

Stuck On Mars, Eating Bars

Me and my bro are on Mars
Stuck on Mars forever
I got hungry so I ate our chocolate bars
They were tasty.

There is so much darkness, nothing bright,
We say, 'Oooh, chocolate.'
I say, 'Come on, let's not fight
Because it's mine.'

'Look,' I say, a superhero, he's super,
'Of course,' Albie says, my bro.
'Oh no,' I said, 'He better not be a party pooper
Because I have a party soon.'

Well, that's my dream... for now!

Harry Fowler (9)
Whybridge Junior School, Rainham

Monster Land

N ow all I can see is spiders everywhere,
I try to find myself in a comfy chair
G etting very nervous, feeling very scared
H orrified that also there are monsters but no chair
T hank goodness for my dad, he's a footballer you know
M aybe he can scare them by shouting, 'Off you go!'
A lso there are dinosaurs walking all around
R oaring in my face and pounding loudly on the ground
E ventually I wake up to find it's just a dream, and my dad is lying next to me.

Harley Millard (9)
Whybridge Junior School, Rainham

Scary Clowns And An Abandoned Circus

On a chilly night, in a deserted place
There stood a man with a weird face
His nose was red and his skin was pale white
He'd give me nightmares any night
I was no harm, my body rigid
But he was angry and livid
I ran fast, I pegged it
My friends close behind
Their screams could be heard as well as mine
He laughed creepily upon us
He was on our tail
Ashton slipped and fell, his knees were weak
As he got dragged by the scary clown
You could hear the echoes of his scream
And was never to be seen.

Luke Shepherd (10)
Whybridge Junior School, Rainham

Unicorn Dream

Look girls! What can you see?
We're up in the sky,
We're above the clouds
Can that be?

Me, Josie and Ruby can dream
But there it was in front of me!
A beautiful unicorn staring at me.

I felt scared,
As I could feel a blizzard on its way
So we all held on tight
We wished for a better day.

To look up and see the blizzard wasn't to be!
There it was in front of me...
A wizard that was taller than me
Will they live happily ever after? Maybe!

Kacie Flatt (9)
Whybridge Junior School, Rainham

Nothing But Space

Where am I? I don't know
Is this a dream? Or a place where stars glow?
Is this a dream?
Or a place where the moons beam?
I am surprised at what my eyes found,
Pink, purple and blue swirls, floating around,
I felt the breeze.
It moved with such ease,
I felt so light,
Everything was so bright,
For once I felt so calm.
Because nothing can reach me and do harm,
I wonder if it is day or night?
But there's one last question, what is this place?
I think it's nothing but space.

Camille Cumlajee (10)
Whybridge Junior School, Rainham

I Love To Eat My Cereal

I love to eat my cereal
In the morning when I wake
Lately it's been Cheerios
Or bowls of Frosted Flakes.

I love to spread some sugar
On Raisin Bran or Life
Apple Jacks are cool to eat,
At eight o'clock at night.

I know I should eat better
To get my morning fuel,
But leaving Fruit Loops off my list
Is downright mean and cruel!

So instead of Cap'n Crunch
Or even Fibre One, I'm eating much more bran
But having much less fun!

Merve Fistikci (11)
Whybridge Junior School, Rainham

Ghost Bus

Underneath the lamppost in the middle of the night, a ghost bus made a silent stop at the bus stop in your corner.
A strange and fearful sight, something big and white climbed down.
It's looking for your bedroom and it has searched all over town
You thought it couldn't find you,
That you were safe and sound.
You thought you could hide where you could never be found.
But now it's here.
You know it loves the scary fright.
There's only one thing you can do,
Quick! Turn on the light!

Kevin Uka (10)
Whybridge Junior School, Rainham

Goblins Invade

G o, go goblins!
O h no! Oh no!
B ring me some gold
L oads! Loads! Loads!
I t could be in a cave
N ot a pile of clothes
S omeone must be guarding it, so careful as you go.

I think I have a plan
N othing can stop us now
V ery quick and very quiet
A nd not long to go now
D efeat is not an option, you've made me proud
E verybody had a prize, come and gather round...

Jae Callender (8)
Whybridge Junior School, Rainham

Famous Flying Princess Lu-Lu

P retty as I may be, I am a fairy
R equest a song, you will get your pay,
I ce is so nice for a rhyming song,
N ice song, ice song, I will let you have a say
C arrots, they play, make me this way
E verything, everyone has a right to dance,
S eeing my kingdom is a pleasure,
S ometimes you only need a little stance.

L ive life,
U sing love
L ove life,
U sing laughter.

Kayleigh Mack (10)
Whybridge Junior School, Rainham

Fantascia!

F antascia is a fantastic place!
A ll the sweets you can eat, the kids find it ace!
N o rules, no adults, it's all about fun
T oday there's an offer on hotdogs, quick! Before there's none
A lot of rides that can make you sick
S creaming out loud! That's the trick!
C andyfloss, gummy bears, lollipops too!
I n fact, that's too much, I need the loo!
A mazing Fantascia! Come here soon.

Mia Fage (10)
Whybridge Junior School, Rainham

Unicorn Dream

L ate on a sunny evening at sunset
A nd running through the breeze,
D ancing and playing through the grass
Y oung, happy and free.

U nder the rise of the moon
N ight-time is here
I lluminated by thousands of stars, I asked
C ould I ride a star, with my unicorn friend
O ver the beautiful moon?
R ainbow lights of the beautiful aurora
N ever ever want this dream to end.

Grace O'Connor (8)
Whybridge Junior School, Rainham

A Dream

A dream can be about anything you want to see,
It could be about a huge dragon,
Or a scary bee.

I wonder how they are made,
While everybody sleeps,
I still wonder that when I wake up,
From my alarm when it beeps.

Are they made from a book
Or produced from a phone?
Once they come to your head
They become your own.

They could be scary, funny or creepy too
What type of dream will happen to you?

Oluwanifemi Femi-Sanni (10)
Whybridge Junior School, Rainham

Nature

Ladybugs on the flowers,
Ladybugs on the corn,
Ladybugs on the leaves,
Ladybugs on the lawn.
Ladybugs in my garden
As hungry as can be
Eating up the aphids,
So something's left for me.

Butterflies on the flowers,
Butterflies on the corn,
Butterflies on the trees,
Butterflies on the lawn.
Butterflies in my garden
As hungry as can be.
Eating up the leaves,
So something's left for me.

Nelie Nunn (10)
Whybridge Junior School, Rainham

Angels Vs Clowns

Stop that, you silly clowns
Leave us alone
Don't scare me, I'm on my way home
I know I'm scared of your faces
Because I see you in many places.

The angels hate you and we have to face you
You killed all of us and you are going to regret it.

You are going to pay for what you did
Do not worry, clowns
You are going to die very soon
Be careful when you are sleeping in your room...

Tommy Young (10)
Whybridge Junior School, Rainham

Summertime

I love to hear the whistle and chime
And watch the birds sit in a line
I love to jump into the pool
Or play a game of football.

As I cannonball
Into our pool,
I think about the splash
With a big crash!

Around here, it's never calm
With birds singing way before my loud alarm
As the sun comes out and the moon goes down
I open my curtains and wake up to my lovely town.

Joseph Croft (10)
Whybridge Junior School, Rainham

Minecraft

M inecraft is a computer game
I like it because I learn as I play
N o two builds are quite the same
E veryone plays it in a different way
C rafting tables are what we use
R edstone is a block you can choose
A rt is what it's all about
F un is all I care about
T ry playing it and you will have no doubt.

Minecraft is the best, I shout.

Kian Shay O'Riordan (10)
Whybridge Junior School, Rainham

Halloween

H alloween is my worst nightmare
A ll around me, ghosts are in the air
L anky, creepy ghosts around the bend
L onging for this dream to end.
O n and on scary faces pass me by
W itches cackling, riding on their broomsticks so high
E erie, petrifying mummies appear
E asily bringing terror to me, oh dear!
N ow finally morning, what a spooky dream I had.

Bobby James Dancer (10)
Whybridge Junior School, Rainham

Danger Awaits!

D reaming through a wonderland
A nd here comes the bad part, but
N o one to be seen.
G argoyles flying, high in the sky
E rupting volcanoes
R un for your life.

A fter that
W aiting is your death
A bove you is sparkling
I n the sky
T winkle, twinkle all through the night
S parkle, sparkle day and night!

Shreya Patel (9)
Whybridge Junior School, Rainham

The Knight

Once upon a time,
There was a knight
And he always got in fights
And always knew what was right.

Once upon a time,
There was a knight
He was afraid of the dark
And got freaked out, whenever a dog barks.

He was fighting the dark
And with all his force, trying to stop the bark
Until one day he met his true love
In his dream, he met just a dove.

Martin Ganchev (10)
Whybridge Junior School, Rainham

The Match

My fellow footballers
Let's win this match
My goalie gets ready to catch
Let's do this for our fans, no time to miss
Pass me the ball, I've got this
I shoot the ball
And the crowd cheers
Then I knew an earthquake is here
The ball flies through the lava and hits the goal
I celebrate and the crowd goes wild
They sing and cheer, 'Go on my child!'

Archie Boys (9)
Whybridge Junior School, Rainham

Killer Clowns

K iller clowns are all about
I n the foggy night
L urking round every corner
L aughing as they scare you
E veryone
R un! Run! Run!

C all the police
L ook around and hide
O h no, I am petrified
W hat am I going to do?
N ow there's sirens all about
S aved by the police.

Katy Leigh Hart (10)
Whybridge Junior School, Rainham

Unicorns... Oh Unicorns

U nreal things are all I can see
N ervous, sweat dripping down my knee
I can see its multicoloured tail
C arefully swirls like a snail
O n its head lays a horn
R un away like Usain Bolt, 'Bye, Mr Unicorn.'
N o! I become dizzy, this is what I always dread
S uddenly I wake up to find I'm safe in bed.

Mosope Braimoh (11)
Whybridge Junior School, Rainham

My Fantastic Dog

Blue Boy is my dog, he can jump high like a frog.
I take him to the fields, so he can sniff the daffodils.
If he sees a rabbit, he will run, run, run.
After our walk, we go back home, I give him a big, juicy bone.
After he goes and curls up on his bed, and rests his tired, sleepy head.
Blue Boy drives me round the bend, but he will always be my best friend.

Jude Smith (8)
Whybridge Junior School, Rainham

Starbright

S uch a beautiful sight
T o see tonight
A lovely colour
R ight in the middle of all the rest
B right and bold
R aining sparkles everywhere
I t's a lovely shape
G ives light when dark
H ides scariness of the dark
T he shooting star is my favourite sight to see tonight.

Lily Bird (9)
Whybridge Junior School, Rainham

The Night Rider

Racing along the tracks, I go
Mud splashing upon my goggles and nose.

Sharp bend approaching, I'm changing gear
My body leans in, I have no fear.

The road sweeps off into the night,
My engine roars, the owls take flight.

The freezing air, it bites my face
As my bike and I disappear without a trace.

George Wescombe (9)
Whybridge Junior School, Rainham

Dancing Dream

All I see is fairies beyond me.
Fluttering by, 1... 2... 3.
Many unicorns around me
And their swirling horns
Sparkling towards me.
Unicorns surrounding me
Their colourful hair grabs my attention.
Their big, curly tails following their trail
Wait, who's behind me?
It's a famous dancer.
Such a good dream!

Ruby Kitching (9)
Whybridge Junior School, Rainham

Untitled

Nowhere to go, nowhere to hide
Where am I? Where shall I bide?
In the forest of dreams,
Helplessly I wander
I am trapped inside, my life is a squander
Everyone sees me as a monster, a threat,
When really I am homeless, cold and wet.
No one wants to look on the inside
And I can't trust anyone. To whom can i confide?

Kian Boot (10)
Whybridge Junior School, Rainham

Useful Unicorns

U nicorns flying through the gorgeous sky
N ear to the Earth and clouds
I t's like we are in a fairytale land
C oming to make us smile
O r maybe to give us hope and joy
R ainbows are their best friends
N o one else believes in them
S miles spread around the world!

Jesse-Jay Olney (10)
Whybridge Junior School, Rainham

Daydreaming But In The Park

I went to the park, on the
Swing I sat
But when I sat, I started
Daydreaming
Like a cat.

I saw Usain Bolt running
For the win
Just like my dad
Looking for a tin.

I saw a footballer
There he goes for a...
Miss!
But I don't really
Like his fists!

Denis Zegheru (9)
Whybridge Junior School, Rainham

Ice Cream Dream

D ad's dreaming of ice cream
R ows and rows of flavoured ice cream
E ggnog is one type of ice cream,
A pricot is another
M any flavours are great
I ce cream comes in all colours
N eopolitan ice cream is my favourite
G reat to dream of ice cream.

Max Chipperfield (8)
Whybridge Junior School, Rainham

Space Rap

Yo, I'm in space, I'm going to my base.
I'm in my rocket and I've got bright stars in my pocket.
I can see spotty, green aliens coming to me,
I feel scared so I'm going to flee.
I'm going to look for my space team.
But then I realised it was a bad dream.

Yeah!

Joshua-James Leach (9)
Whybridge Junior School, Rainham

My Forest Nightmare

My forest nightmare gave me an absolute scare
Dolls appeared as creepy as ever
Trees shook wildly, oh my god, the weather!
The storm was frightful, the opposite of delightful
We ran into a crowd, where mad people frowned.
Me and my brother, yes we were lost,
I wouldn't go back, at any cost.

Lara Crandle (8)
Whybridge Junior School, Rainham

Orcas And Me

I wish I was an orca, I would swim all day at sea.
I wish I was an orca, then they wouldn't eat me.
I wish I was an orca, I would sing a lovely song.
I wish I was an orca, I would be very long.
I wish I was an orca, it would be my time.
I wish I was an orca, I would have a lovely rhyme.

Oliver Maynard (9)
Whybridge Junior School, Rainham

How To Find Mythical Fairies

Some mythical fairies live under the sea,
If you don't believe me, go and see!

Go down the beach and in the tide,
If you don't believe me, go ask Clyde.

You'll find a dolphin further along,
If you don't find one, you've read it wrong!

Holly Landers (10)
Whybridge Junior School, Rainham

Dreams

D eep in the night, dreaming away
R estless and sleepy from my busy school day
E very night, my imagination runs wild, but this time
A wizard gives me a mystery wind dial
M agical dust, spread in a rush,
S leepy head, it's time for bed.

Ashton Hind (10)
Whybridge Junior School, Rainham

Wizard

W hooshing through the air on a broom,
I n and out of the soft white clouds I zoom,
Z igzagging here and zigzagging there,
A wizard appears from out of nowhere,
R oaring and rearing as fierce as can be,
D ragon is coming, please help me!

Freya Barnard (10)
Whybridge Junior School, Rainham

Me And My Cloud

Once upon a time,
A little boy did climb
Up the highest mountain
Where snow flows like a fountain
A cold breeze
Strokes your hair
Where there's music
In the air!
Clouds waving from the sky
Give him his wings and let
Him fly!

Chelvathurai Thanuzsan Thiruchelvam (9)
Whybridge Junior School, Rainham

Betrayed

I'm here forever
I didn't know what to do
Prisoner I was.

Locked up... ages now
He betrayed us, oh how sad.
Seeking revenge.

But that's no good, see.
Now I solved the mystery
It's dear to me now...

Erika Wilkins (9)
Whybridge Junior School, Rainham

What Mum Said

'Come on,' said Mum,
'It's time for bed.
PJs on, you sleepy head.
Sweet dreams for you,' said Mum,
Little did she know
How I dread,
Having to go to bed,
Just in case something scary
Jumped into my head.

Sydney Stiffel (11)
Whybridge Junior School, Rainham

Spiders Are Scary

S cary and hairy
P articularly the big ones give me a fright
I n the dark of night
D arkness hides them
E erie shadows across my ceiling
R eally give me a creepy feeling
S piders are scary!

Sadie Williams (9)
Whybridge Junior School, Rainham

Candy Land

All I see before me is pink trees, candy springs
A wonderful mouth-watering delight
Candyfloss clouds, jelly bean flowers
Along with cocoa grass and lemon grass.

Make tonight the last night in our wonderful land of candy land.

Sky Wood (9)
Whybridge Junior School, Rainham

Waffles

W affles are the best with syrup
A ll you can eat
F ind it wherever you go
F ull of love and joy
L ovely, smooth, rich centre
E veryday life forever
S yrup is the best with waffles.

Jason Kissi Koranteng (10)
Whybridge Junior School, Rainham

The Chicken Dinner

On my plate, ready to eat
Sometimes a chicken dinner can be a treat.
Have it in a roast or a burger bun.
Go crazy with the ketchup, make it fun.
Thinking about the chicken, now it's dead
It think I will have beef instead!

Alby Buttery (8)
Whybridge Junior School, Rainham

Super Dream

I am walking my dog,
When I see birds in the sky,
I wish I could fly,
Now the park is empty
We both start to rise
Yes, we are flying
What a wonderful sight
Oh what a wonderful view!

Nanupriya Bhandari (8)
Whybridge Junior School, Rainham

Jigglypuff!

Just a peep of her song
You will be asleep all day long
Her cute little eyes
Will give you no surprise
Dancing in the sun
Having lots of fun.

That's what Jigglypuff does.

Rosie Casey (11)
Whybridge Junior School, Rainham

Football Fun

H aving fun, playing football
A lways slide tackling,
R acing to the ball,
R ound the pitch I go,
Y ay, I just scored!

Harry Casey (11)
Whybridge Junior School, Rainham

Creeping Clown

C reeping you out
L ooming about
O ut in the wild
W here nobody goes
N ever be spotted
S o watch out!

Sumaya Yesmin (9)
Whybridge Junior School, Rainham

I Dream

I dream, I run
It is so fun
I dream, I swim
I have to win
I dream, I jump
Oops!
I fell out of bed with a thump.

Ava-May Watts (9)
Whybridge Junior School, Rainham

Est.1991

YOUNG WRITERS INFORMATION

We hope you have enjoyed reading this book – and that you will continue to in the coming years.

If you're a young writer who enjoys reading and creative writing, or the parent of an enthusiastic poet or story writer, do visit our website **www.youngwriters.co.uk**. Here you will find free competitions, workshops and games, as well as recommended reads, a poetry glossary and our blog.

If you would like to order further copies of this book, or any of our other titles, then please give us a call or visit **www.youngwriters.co.uk**.

Young Writers
Remus House
Coltsfoot Drive
Peterborough
PE2 9BF
(01733) 890066
info@youngwriters.co.uk